This book belongs to:

_____

The Worry Warrior

This book was inspired by my wonderful daughter
and our pet dog, Rosie.

Disclaimer: This book does not provide medical advice.
This book is for educational and informational purposes only and does not constitute
medical advice. Readers should consult their doctor or a qualified healthcare
professional for medical advice or specific healthcare questions.

Printed in United Kingdom.
Lavender Press.
ISBN: 9780993487972.

For fun free activities and helpful resources
visit: hpcarr.com/rosie

There was a puppy named Rosie,
Who loved to snuggle up cozy.
With big brown eyes and fox-red fur,
She loved it when people cuddled her.

Rosie was happy every day,
She loved to run free and play.

As Rosie grew, she learned new rules.
The time soon came for Puppy School.

Suddenly, the worries started to grow
Like a monster in her mind, she felt low.

Rosie didn't like feeling full of doubt

She wanted to try and figure it out.

Rosie longed for confidence and cheer,
But instead, worry made her feel fear.
She wanted to find a way to feel jollier,
To turn from a worrier into a warrior.

The journey began with a wise old hound,
Sharing a secret that was quite profound.

"To conquer worries, Rosie dear,
Be brave and bold and face your fear."

"Take a deep breath, then let it all go,
Imagine filling a balloon as you blow.

When it's full of worries, blow it away,
Make it stop with a pop and save the day."

"Fear and excitement feel the same,
You have the power to reframe.

How you feel is down to you,
There's nothing that you cannot do."

"Now, close your eyes and imagine it clear,
How would you feel if worry disappeared?

Focus on how you want to feel instead.
Feel it in your body, imagine it in your head."

"When you focus on what you want to be,
That's how you create your reality.

You become what you believe to be true;
What you believe is true becomes true to you."

Climbing a mountain of doubt, Rosie stood tall,
Even when her worries tried to make her fall.
One step at a time is how she progressed,
Little by little, test by test.

"I am a worry warrior; have no fear."
Rosie's voice was loud and clear.
Rosie's heart was full of hope,
She knew that she could always cope.

Starting school was a dream come true,
She learned so many things she could do.

She found the teachers were really kind,
Nothing was as scary as it seemed in her mind.

Rosie's tale can inspire us all,
To conquer worries, stand strong and tall.
You too can break through any barrier,
Learning the ways of the Worry Warrior.

Transform From a Worrier to a Warrior

Have you ever felt worried? Everyone feels that way sometimes. Even the most super successful and confident people you can think of felt nervous and had to overcome worries at some point.

Fear is our body's way of trying to keep us safe and comfortable. However, feeling the fizz of nervous excitement can also be a good sign that we are learning and developing new skills by trying new things.

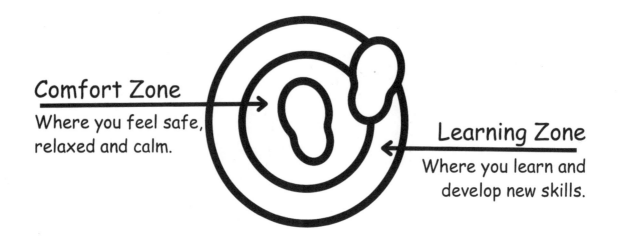

Comfort Zone
Where you feel safe, relaxed and calm.

Learning Zone
Where you learn and develop new skills.

Worry Warriors have learned how to understand their fears and focus on their strengths and superpowers. With the following five exercises, you can learn the ways of the Worry Warrior too! ✓

Remember, you are unique and brilliant. When you try your best and feel your best, you can give your best and get the best results.

1. Feel How Good it Feels to Feel Good

Imagine feeling strong, brave, happy, healthy, and confident. How good would it be to really feel all of these things? One by one, imagine being each of them right now. What does it feel like in your body?

"What you believe to be true becomes true to you."

Conceive > Believe > Achieve.

When you tell your mind what you want, you can make your mind up to make that happen. Say how you want to feel as if it were true right now. For example, if you want to feel brave, say, "I am brave!" These become positive power statements you can use to focus on what you want.

⊘ Write out a list of positive power statements and say them often.

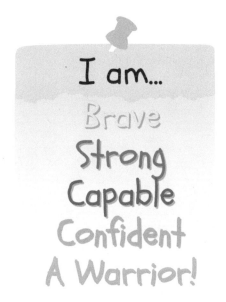

I am...
Brave
Strong
Capable
Confident
A Warrior!

2. The Power of Truth

Sometimes, we worry about things that aren't actually true. We make up stories about ideas that may (or may not) happen in the future.

When you worry, ask yourself — is that really true — right now?

For example, Rosie's worry - "What if I'm not liked?" She could not know this before she's even met the new people, it's a "what if... worry." Instead, Rosie could think about all the people that do, in fact, like her. Then she has proof of the truth. She has the power to stop the worry by focussing on what she knows to be true right now.

How many "what if... worries" can you think of to challenge or change?

3. Let Go Of Things You Cannot Control

Worries tend to be about things that have already happened in the past, or *might* happen in the future, which we can't change or control.

Instead, focus on what you CAN control, like your thoughts and actions. Here's an activity to help you let go of the things you cannot control.

☑ Take a piece of paper and divide it into what you can/cannot control.

Can Control
Myself
How I respond
What I focus on

Cannot Control
The past
The future
Other people

Break your worry down into lists of things you can control, and let go of anything you cannot change — cross it out, rip it up and recycle it!

If you focus on what you CAN do, you'll be able to find solutions much easier (without wasting time or energy on the things you can't control).

There's always a solution to every problem - you just have to find it. If you have a problem, ask what can you do to help find a solution. What ONE action can you choose to take now that is within your control?

4. Speak Your Body's Language

Feelings are the language of your body. You can change how you feel by communicating with your body through your breath.

When it comes to letting go of worries, take a deep breath in through your nose and fill your belly with air. Blow out through your mouth to feel calmer. You can imagine filling up a balloon. Release the air and any worries from your body as you blow the worry-balloon up and away, or pretend to pop it and stop it for good!

✅ Another relaxing breathing exercise you can try is square breaths.

Imagine drawing a square of four sides with your breath.
   1. Breathe in for a count of 4,
   2. Hold for 4,
   3. Breathe out for 4,
   4. Hold for 4.

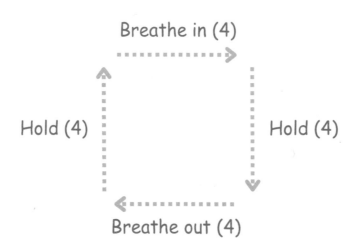

Breathe in (4)

Hold (4)   Hold (4)

Breathe out (4)

5. Strike a Power Pose!

How do you think a Warrior or Superhero looks? Confident, powerful, strong? They often stand in what is called a "power pose."

How many power poses can you do?
1. Thumbs up. Arms up high.
2. Punch the air with your fist.
3. Arms confidently crossed in front of you.
4. Feet apart firmly on the floor. Hands on hips.
5. Showing off your arm muscles with a bicep curl.

When you stand confidently, not only do you look more confident to others, but you will feel more confident too.

To make it extra powerful, say your positive statements, such as: "I am confident, I am brave, I am strong. I am capable. I am a warrior!"

☑ Try it and see how you feel before and after on a scale of 1-10.

Thank You For Reading
Rosie The Worry Warrior

Thank you for helping Rosie find her superpowers as a Worry Warrior.

Congratulations on developing your own skills and superpowers. You can use these tools anytime, anywhere, to break through worry and feel your best.

Focus on what you want and how you wish to feel. Use your imagination to communicate with your mind, and your breath and power-poses to communicate with your body. Focus on what you can control and release what you cannot. You have the power.

You are the hero of your life's story and the best you in the world. 🌍

Go to hpcarr.com/rosie for free fun activities.

SCAN ME

Milton Keynes UK
Ingram Content Group UK Ltd.
UKHW050907080624
443694UK00003BB/19